Let It RIP!

David and Nick have a secret.

But this is no

ordinary secret.

It's a fart

in a jar for kids to use.

It's how to stop being bored…

Let It RIP!

David and Nick have the smelliest plan of all!

Archimede Fusillo

Illustrated by Stephen Michael King

PHILADELPHIA·LONDON

For my children, Laurence and Alyssa. *A.F.*
For Stinky O'Keefe. *S.M.K.*

Library of Congress Control Number: 2005928814

ISBN-13: 978-0-7624-2622-5
ISBN-10: 0-7624-2622-5

Original design by David Altheim and Ruth Grüner, Penguin Design Studio.
Additional design for this edition by Frances J. Soo Ping Chow

Typography: Machine, MetaPlus, and New Century School Book

This book may be ordered by mail from the publisher.
Please include $2.50 for postage and handling.
But try your bookstore first!

This edition published by Running Press Kids, an imprint of
Running Press Book Publishers
125 South Twenty-second Street
Philadelphia, Pennsylvania 19103-4399

Visit us on the web!
www.runningpress.com

Ages 7–10
Grades 2–4

ONE

"Are you sure this works?"

It was Mustard, asking the same question for the hundredth time. He was new at the school and didn't really know too much about me and my farts.

"Would I lie to you?" asked my best friend Nick.

But Mustard still looked more than a bit unsure.

"Give me the jar," I said, and grabbed it out of Mustard's hand.

"I'll prove to you it works."

And saying that I crossed the school yard to where a gaggle of Grade Six girls were sitting in a circle. I knew Mustard would be watching me so I made a real show of opening the lid of the jar.

The girls looked at me, not knowing what to think.

"See that guy over there," I said quietly. I turned and pointed at Mustard, but not so he could see me doing it. "That guy there wants to give each of you girls a big mushy kiss. Who wants to be first?"

It worked great. The girls took one look at Mustard's face and almost puked on the spot. I mean, who wouldn't?

Mustard's face looks like he's spent too much time running into parked cars. I wasn't going to waste a perfectly good fart just because Mustard wanted proof that he was getting the real thing.

"Well," I chimed when I returned to

3

Mustard and Nick. "What do you think now?" I said, making a show of closing the already closed lid on the jar really tightly.

Mustard's eyes said it all. He was in. Hook, line, and stinker.

"Give us four jars," he panted. "Nah, better make it six . . . Maybe seven. Yeah,

seven jars. My sister's got a sleepover and this'll make having all those girls around the house more bearable."

Mustard went to take the jar from my hands but I clutched it to my chest.

"Look, I dunno about it now, Mustard," I said slowly. "I mean, we were willing to

sell you our best jar but you wouldn't take our word for it." I shook my head dramatically.

Nick prodded me. "He wants seven jars," he said stiffly.

"You gotta sell me the jars," Mustard pleaded. "I just wanted to be certain, that's all." There was slight panic in his voice.

"Dave," Nick whispered in my ear, "Dave, he wants seven jars. We've only got two. This and the one in my bag."

I ignored Nick and faced Mustard.

"Did you see those girls scatter when I let them have just a tiny whiff of the stuff in that jar?" I asked. "This is my personal jar, Mustard. I made it, so to speak."

Mustard fumbled in
his pocket and came out
with five dollars. "Here,
take this. I'll give you the rest when I get
the other five jars."

I curled my bottom lip and narrowed
my eyes like I was really concentrating.

"Just this once, Mustard," I said finally.
"Next time you doubt me, I'm blacklisting
you from buying any more Fart in a Jar."

Mustard beamed and took the jar
from me.

"Remember to read the instructions
before you use the jar," I called out
as Mustard ran off. "We won't take any
responsibility if you mess it up!"

Nick was scratching his head. "We've gotta find five more jars," he announced.

"No problemo," I answered. "I got Mom to make me some hot salami and Italian relish sandwiches. A few of those and watch out!"

Nick squirmed.

Hot salami and Italian relish were a deadly combination when taken by someone like me. Why? Because I have this gift of being able to fart on cue.

I discovered my talent in Grade Three during a particularly boring reading lesson, sitting there on the floor

next to Hazel Pettula.

She loved to hear the

sound of her own voice

as she read out loud.

I must have wanted to

drown out her voice or

something because I gave out with one

of the loudest and longest farts in history.

I mean my fart was just like one very

long, very loud burst from a train whistle,

except smellier, much much smellier.

Think of the worst smell you have ever

smelt and multiply it by a zillion.

Now you have *half* the strength

of my farts on a good day, when I can

9

clear an entire school hall. On a bad day I can clear a classroom without even trying.

And so, a short time later, after my mom's hot salami and relish sandwiches, I got to work making up Mustard's remaining five jars.

TWO

The idea for Fart in a Jar was mine. It was too easy for me to fart on cue when we were bored in class or we wanted to rile a substitute teacher. But I could only ever drop one good one in one location at any one time. The kids lucky enough to be around me at the time got all the benefits.

Like the time we had a surprise Math test. Miss Walters just waltzed into the classroom, started handing out reams of paper, and announced that we were

having a pop quiz to see who had

bothered to learn any of the work from

the past week. Well, I just closed my eyes,

focused on the task, and let rip with

a Force 3 fart.

Farts are measured on a scale of 1 to

5. Force 1 is just a little hiccup fart,

the kind old grannies might do when
they're sitting on a bus and don't
want to disturb anyone. Force 1 farts
are harmless, hardly worth measuring.
A Force 3 fart sounds like a car
backfiring, short and sharp, but loud
enough to make those around you jump.

If you're ever around when a Force 5 goes down, well, you don't want to be is all I can say.

Unlike a Force 1 fart, a Force 3 fart can only be controlled by an expert. It takes practice to release the fart so that it comes out in bursts, like a series of trumpet blasts.

On the day of the Math test, I was sitting at the back of the class as usual.

I waited until Miss Walters was at her desk before I got myself into gear. By the time the third trumpet had sounded, Nancy Wong, who was sitting in front of me, couldn't take any more and begged Miss Walters to let her leave her desk for some fresh air.

At first Miss Walters ignored Nancy, told her not to be silly, but as the first whiffs reached her desk, Miss Walters' composure broke down, bit by bit.

"It's just an odd smell, dear," Miss Walters tried at first. "Don't let it worry you."

It took the fifth blast of my Force 3 to get Miss Walters to close her eyes and grimace, but it was worth the effort.

outside!

A minute later Miss Walters had the entire class outside, the doors and windows open to let fresh air into the room, and the quiz was all but forgotten.

I was a legend after that episode. Or rather, my farting on cue was legendary.

By lunchtime, everyone who was having Miss Walters' pop quiz wanted me to sit next to them.

And so Fart in a Jar was born.

THREE

The idea for Fart in a Jar just flashed into my head, the way really good ideas do. I saw me, a container, a puff of smoke, and people running with their hands cupped over their noses. Brilliant.

Problem was, though, that getting the idea and actually following through on it were two different things.

Like any genius inventor, I had to try all sorts of ways to make my idea work. The main problem was packaging. At first I tried Fart in a Can, but that didn't work

because I couldn't seal the cans properly.
Besides, cans were rather too brittle for
my big Force 5s.

Next I tried airtight containers from
out of Mom's pantry. But they were no
good because a really good fart could
blast the container totally out of shape,
and maybe even puncture it.

18

It was Nick who came up with the idea of the jars.

"The farts will probably keep fresh for a while in jars," Nick gushed. "We can even make up some fancy labels to whack on them too. Maybe write down a few instructions on how to get the best results."

"What about a list of ingredients?" I added. I liked the idea of people being able to store my product for future use.

By the time Mustard ordered seven jars of Fart in a Jar, Nick and I were the Fart Kings of Fitzroy North, the undisputed Fart Fiends of the neighborhood.

And we could have grown bigger too. Maybe even gone statewide, perhaps national, and later on become global. Nick and I had started looking at franchise opportunities and perhaps running weekend seminars for kids to come and learn the art of farting in a jar.

We had to do something because demand was starting to outstrip supply and we didn't want to let anyone down. There was no way I was going to give out my secrets on how to get the best out of a fart, but I figured that if kids were going to copy me, I might as well be in on the action from the start. Besides, if I made farting in a jar look difficult, kids might be reluctant to have a go on their own for fear of splinters and unexpected afterburn.

You do have to be very careful, almost scientific, with the manufacturing of a Fart in a Jar. Not just anyone can do it.

That's why I was in charge of manufacturing and Nick was in charge of distribution. Nick had contacts at all sorts of schools in our area, and if he wanted to, I think Nick could sell bottled sunshine to people living in the tropics.

Nick and I had a great thing going. We sold stacks of Fart in a Jar every week, especially on Fridays when kids had to visit their parents' boring friends

during the weekend, or they had to watch
their younger sister in a dance competi-
tion or their brother at a football game.
Fart in a Jar saved heaps of kids from
being bored to death.

At the rate Nick and I were
moving Fart in a Jar, we were going to
be millionaires before we finished
Grade Five.

But that was before my grandmother
decided to stay with us while her own
house was being painted and recarpeted.

FOUR

My grandmother is a terrific cook. She
makes her own pasta and has all sorts of
secret ingredients she doesn't share with
anyone, not even Mom.

"You look very tired, David," she
said to me the first night we sat down
to dinner together. "Maybe you're not
eating properly."

"Nah, I'm fine," I told her. I smiled
thinly and poked at the peas on my plate.
My grandmother was right, I was tired.
And sore. Just that afternoon Nick and

I had had to fill a huge order for Fart in a
Jar for his cousin Wilma. Her school was
having an assembly to present the sports
awards and Wilma had wanted twelve
Force 4 jars, one for each of her friends
to unleash during the ceremony.

"I should make you some of my special

soup," my grandmother continued. "It's full of beans and carrots and celery. Even a little bit of garlic. It will perk you up, no worries."

I was about to tell my grandmother that I wasn't a soup kind of guy when the phone rang. It was Nick. He sounded desperate.

"Wilma's in trouble," Nick announced. "She dropped

most of the jars by accident and now she's short."

"Dropped them!" I screeched. "I thought you told her she had to be extra careful with them."

"I did, but they fell out of her school bag as she got out of her mom's car. The jars shattered all over my auntie's driveway and Wilma thinks the entire house is blanketed in a cloud of your, well, you know."

I could see it now. Clouds of greenish-
yellow mist billowing everywhere. Nine
Force 4s! Even *I* had never been around
when a heap of Force 4s had been
unleashed together. I'd hate to have been
Wilma and her mom when they caught
a whiff.

"Davo," Nick pleaded, "you've got to
come up with the replacements."

"I can't right now. Not Force 4s
anyway," I answered.

"I've got some week-old fish heads I
can bring round to your place. You can
munch on those and see how you go,"
Nick offered helpfully. "You've got to help
me out."

I smelt a rat. "Why? What's so
desperate about replacing your cousin's
jars?"

There was silence down the line for a
few moments. Then when Nick did speak
his voice was squeaky.

"I've already spent the money she gave us for the jars," he whispered. "If I don't replace the jars, Wilma's going to let on to Dad about Fart in a Jar."

It was my turn to be silent. One of the reasons Fart in a Jar was so successful was that no one ever let on about it to adults. It was *our* secret,

our weapon against having to be bored out of our brains.

"Davo? Davo, I'm sorry. I just couldn't help myself."

I didn't answer. Instead, I hung up and went back to the kitchen table.

"What did you say is in your soup?" I asked my grandmother as casually as I could. "Do you think you could whip some up for me now? I really could use a pick-me-up."

FIVE

Lucky for me my grandmother is one of
those people who loves to make others
happy. It wasn't long before I had a huge
bowl of steaming soup in front of me.

Beans and carrots. Thousands of them
floating in the broth. There was
enough ammunition there
for me to manufacture
a hundred jars, and
then some.

"Eat up," my grandmother said. And I
did. I ate three bowls. Not because I was

hungry, but I figured that if one bowl of this wind-laden soup would help me fill Wilma's order, then three would give me material to make up a few extras and get a head start on any new orders. Carrots, you see, give me wind. And beans, well . . .

I worked hard after that to refill Wilma's order. I tried for Force 4s but couldn't avoid the odd Force 5.

If I was tired before, I was exhausted now. By the time I phoned Nick to collect the jars, I was ready to collapse into bed.

"You're a real friend," Nick beamed
when he saw the new batch lined up on
the windowsill of my bedroom.

I was too sore to answer.

Next morning, filled with confidence,
I grabbed four jars off the windowsill and
headed for school.

Nick was waiting for me at the bus

stop as usual. "Thanks for last night," he said right away.

"Yeah well, maybe we'd better tell customers that we're not replacing any jars they break or lose."

Nick nodded so hard I thought his head was going to come loose. "Sure thing, Davo."

Mustard was on the bus when Nick and I scrambled aboard.

"So, how'd it go?" I asked him. I liked to get feedback on the product.

The corners of Mustard's mouth turned up and he half closed his eyes.

"Wicked. Just wicked," he said finally. "I took the jars and scattered them around the house before my sister's friends arrived for the sleepover, right. I put them all over the place. Anywhere the girls were going to hang out. Then, when my sister and her friends were all cozy and comfy, I got a friend of mine to help me unscrew the lids and let the vapors free."

Mustard laughed and slapped his knees. "The stench was awesome," he cried. "It was like someone had let loose about a trillion really bad eggs!"

I smiled. I liked good reports.

"You should have seen the look on their faces when the girls got a good whiff of the stench!" Mustard reported. "At first they just sort of looked at each other. It was like no one wanted to admit there was a smell. They just sort of tried to ignore it. At first my sister just turned up her nose and smiled, but then she started blinking and wiping the end of her nose like there was a booger there or something. But she couldn't pretend for too long, and pretty soon even my folks had to leave! It was beautiful. The house was cleared of girls and their giggles in no time flat!"

Nick smiled and high-fived me. I was

blown away. After all, Mustard had only had Force 3 farts, maybe just one Force 4, but certainly no Force 5s.

I pictured with pleasure how Wilma's Force 5s would go down at her school assembly. A real stinkeroo, that's how!

I tried to imagine what my grandmother would do if she knew how I had put her best and most secret soup to work.

SIX

My grandmother wouldn't have been too impressed. I opened one of my jars in the back seat of the school bus.

Mustard, Nick, and I then made for the front door and got out of the bus. We stood just outside waiting for the driver's reaction once the fumes reached him.

"Don't stare," I said to Mustard, who was eyeing the driver intently. "You don't want him to get suspicious, do you?"

Mustard shook his head.

40

The bus driver gave us a nod and the door hissed shut.

"I must have released a Force 5," I said to Nick, explaining the lack of reaction from the driver. Force 5 farts are heavier than the others and so they travel a lot slower. "He probably won't get the full impact until the bus gets to the gate," I added with a shrug. "Pity. I would love

to have seen the look on his face when he got a noseful."

The three of us walked off without sparing the bus driver another thought.

"Do you ever catch a whiff yourself when you're filling the jars?" Mustard asked suddenly.

"Not really," I answered. "In the early

days I did, sure, heaps of times. I was
too slow getting the lid on, or I slipped.
I'm super-efficient nowadays, and I
haven't been hit with the stench in ages."
I lowered my voice. "It's an art, Mustard.
A craft."

Mustard nodded. He was really thick
sometimes.

Nick wasn't saying anything. He was walking just ahead of me and Mustard.

"Nick gets hit with it sometimes though, don't you, Nick?" I said. Mustard laughed. "Now and then I let one go without warning, or Nick's standing too close."

I laughed. Mustard laughed even louder. Nick kept walking.

It was only when we got to our lockers that Mustard went off to join his friends.

"You do get hit with it sometimes," I said to Nick, who seemed to be moping. "Not as often as you used to. Not like when we first started."

"Something's not right," Nick

announced when we'd gathered our books
for the first two periods and were about
to head off for our classroom.

"What do you mean?"

"Well, in the bus before," Nick
answered. "Even a Force 5 fart should
have wafted to the front of the bus by the
time it pulled out."

I slapped Nick on the
shoulder and spun him
round towards the
classroom. "You think I'm losing my
touch?" It wasn't a serious question.

Nick shook his head.

"Tell you what, Nicko," I said, reaching
into my school bag and fishing out the
smallest of the remaining jars, an old
jam jar. "Why don't we let this one go
right now?"

Nick's eyes lit up. "What? Here?"

I shook my head. "This way," I said,
and off I went, in the opposite direction
from our classroom.

SEVEN

"Excuse me," I said in my best voice, pushing open the staff room door, "Excuse me. We were told to take this to the staff room." I held the jar up so that my hand covered most of the label. "It's for the teachers' morning tea. The ladies in the cafeteria told us to put it in the staff room."

Beside me Nick froze. I felt the ice tickle my skin. We had never delivered a Fart in a Jar to the staff room before, directly or otherwise.

I pushed the door to the staff room open a little wider. Just as I'd expected, the room was empty. All the teachers were either in class already or still on hall duty.

"Come on," I snapped and pulled Nick inside.

"You're nuts," Nick told me as I led him towards the kitchen sink, near which there was a toaster and an assortment of spreads.

Quickly I made room for my jar amongst the jars of jam and peanut butter and cookies.

"What're you doing, Dave?"

"I can't just leave this lying in the open, can I?" I answered. "That would be too obvious."

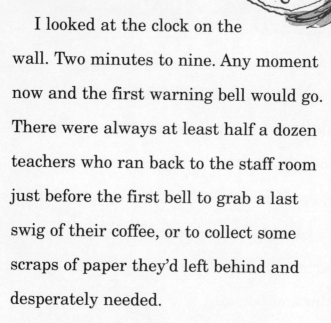

I looked at the clock on the wall. Two minutes to nine. Any moment now and the first warning bell would go. There were always at least half a dozen teachers who ran back to the staff room just before the first bell to grab a last swig of their coffee, or to collect some scraps of paper they'd left behind and desperately needed.

"Just a few seconds more," I whispered. And then, just as the warning bell sounded, I unscrewed the lid of my jar

and bolted for the door, dragging Nick

with me into the corridor.

Nick wanted to get as far away from

the staff room as fast as he could but I

grabbed him.

"Just wait for one or two of the

teachers to go in there," I whispered.

"Where's the fun unless we can see their

reaction?" I had a thought that made me smile. "You wouldn't want to be the first teacher in there," I said. "Imagine what the other teachers would think you'd done if you were the only one standing there."

Nick shook his head but I saw him grin. I was hoping the jar had held at least a Force 4 fart.

"'Good morning, gentlemen."

The voice made Nick and me jump.

"Shouldn't you boys be in class?"

It was the Principal, Mrs. Greenaway. She was behind us, coffee mug in hand.

"We had to run an errand to the office, Mrs. Greenaway," I offered, because Nick had gone white.

Mrs. Greenaway looked me and Nick over for a moment then shooed us away. Nick and I turned to go, but not before we watched the Principal enter the staff room, followed a few seconds later by a Grade Five teacher and the gym teacher.

I think Nick and I laughed all the way
to our first class, and through most of the
first two periods.

Ours is a pretty small school, and both
Nick and I wondered how long it would
be before word filtered out about the
stink in the staff room.

But word never came. Not even by
lunchtime when Nick and I had started
dropping hints to other students about

what we'd done. Of course they didn't believe us. They were waiting for proof.

We waited right through to the end of the day, but by this time Nick and I decided we knew what had happened: Mrs. Greenaway had made the others swear to silence about what they had found or risk losing their jobs. Even if she knew she hadn't farted, Mrs. Greenaway had no way of proving otherwise to the others, and it must have been so embarrassing for her anyway to be caught in a room reeking with what I hoped was at least a Force 4 fart.

EIGHT

"Do you think Greenaway will connect me and you with the smell in the staff room?"

I looked at Nick and frowned. He worried too much.

"What? Just because me and you were standing outside the staff room?" I replied. "Relax."

I was feeling pretty good because word had got around about how well Fart in a Jar had gone at Mustard's sister's sleepover. All through lunch Nick and I

had taken orders from kids wanting to

get hold of jars.

"Lucky I made up that extra batch last

night," I said as Nick sorted out the

orders, giving those who had paid

up-front first pick. "I think I might be

eating soup again
tonight," I laughed.

By the time we got
to Nick's front door
Nick and I had counted
twelve orders, not
including Mustard's
new order for five
more jars.

"We're going to be
short on jars soon,"
I told Nick. Our moms
must have thought
that Nick and I had
a thing for any food
that came in a jar

because we polished it
off so quickly. Truth
was, most of the
original contents got
washed down the sink.

"Perhaps we should
start telling people
that they need to get
the jars back to us once
they've used the
contents," I suggested.
"What we can do is give
them a discount on
their next order for
returning the jars.
Maybe as an incentive

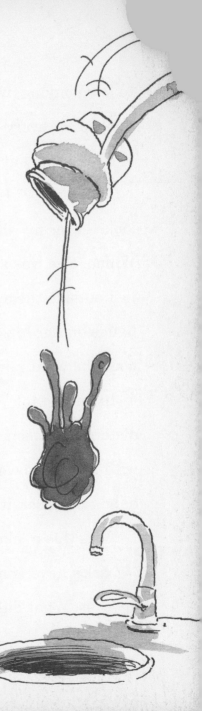

to keep buying, we could give away a free Force 4 for every six jars bought."

Nick looked at me, then past me.

"What's up?" I asked. I turned and looked over my shoulder. There was Wilma. She was standing on the landing just outside the apartment Nick lived in, hands on her hips, nostrils flared. "What does she want now?"

In an instant Wilma crossed the short distance between us and stood toe to toe with Nick. She was holding a jar in her hand and shook it in Nick's face.

"Was this a joke?" she screeched.

Nick's head snapped back. I narrowed my eyes. What did she think Fart in a

Jar was? A science project? Of course it

was a joke!

"Take a whiff!" Wilma demanded and,

twisting the top off the jar, held it out

towards first Nick and then me, both of

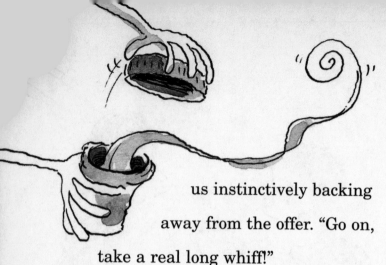

us instinctively backing away from the offer. "Go on, take a real long whiff!"

Wilma seemed to be all blurred arms and legs as she grabbed jar after jar out of her school bag and offered each in turn for me and Nick to smell.

"You owe me bigtime, Nick," Wilma snapped and waved her fist at her cousin. "You and your friend here made me look like a deadset idiot at assembly."

I could see Nick was a little stunned at the

outburst so I stepped
forward and grabbed two
jars out of Wilma's hands.

Carefully I sniffed one, then the other,
closing my eyes in preparation for the
lingering stench.

"Fartfest!" Wilma cried. "That's what
you said it'd be, Nick. A fartfest!"

"Nick!" I managed before Wilma
rounded on me.

"You guys owe me
my money back,"
she spat. "If I wanted
fragrances,
I would have
bought flowers

and waved those about at assembly!"

I held the jars up to Nick's nose. At first he hesitated but I shoved the jars closer and Nick took a short whiff.

"I don't understand," I whispered.

Instead of making my eyes water, gagging me and making me want to run for cover, what lingered in the jars was a slightly sweet and pleasant aroma.

"You don't understand! You don't understand! How do you think I felt when the hall ended up smelling like a botanic garden!" Wilma slapped a hand to her forehead. "Fartfest, my butt!"

I didn't know what to say. I just stared
at Nick and he just stared at the empty
jars. Something had gone horribly wrong.
Something had failed. And that something
could only be *ME!*

"The staff room," Nick whispered finally.

"The bus this morning," I added as
a light went on in my brain.

The jars Wilma had shoved at us.
The ones Nick had collected from
me the night before. They were
all from the same batch as the
ones I'd taken to school that morning.

My heart sank. My knees wobbled.

"I've gotta go," I called as
I ran for the street,

leaving Nick to deal with Wilma.

I had a cold dread about what might

have happened.

NINE

I opened all the remaining jars on the windowsill of my bedroom. Not one Force 4 amongst them. No Force 1s even. I slumped on my bed, the aroma from the jars slowly filling the air around me.

This was a disaster. Had I lost my touch?

I couldn't explain it.

For some reason my farts from the previous night were pleasant.

I concentrated.

I farted.

I sniffed.

My eyes didn't water, my mouth didn't become parched, my legs didn't wobble. There was just this fragrant aroma in the room.

I tried again. And again. And again, until I was almost too sore to sit down.

Overnight I'd gone from being able

to produce Force 5s capable of levelling
a small building to this!

I was almost beside myself when I
heard my grandmother whistling from
the kitchen. Only then did it occur to me
that the sudden change might be a result
of her soup. But that didn't make sense
because my grandmother's soup was
made up of all the best things to give me
maximum fart potential.

A second later and I was scrambling to the kitchen. "What's in your soup?" I asked without a reason.

My grandmother looked up at me. She smiled. "You're back from school," she announced, like this would be news to me.

"Your soup. What's in it?"

My grandmother sat back in her chair

and stopped rolling out the pasta sheet. She was up to her elbows in flour.

"Carrots, peas, broccoli, broad beans, brown beans," she began. "Why do you ask?"

I scratched my head. I was sweating. "Anything else?" I asked, because I knew how she always had secret ingredients in everything she cooked.

My grandmother tapped her lips gently, tiny puffs of flour spitting out between her fingers. "Not too much more," she said finally.

"But there is something else, right?" I pressed.

My grandmother nodded, "Of course.

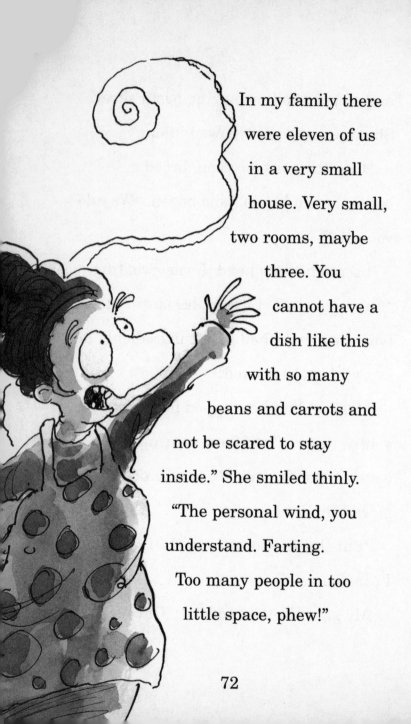

In my family there were eleven of us in a very small house. Very small, two rooms, maybe three. You cannot have a dish like this with so many beans and carrots and not be scared to stay inside." She smiled thinly. "The personal wind, you understand. Farting. Too many people in too little space, phew!"

I half closed my eyes.

"Farting was a problem then?" I asked softly, afraid of the answer.

My grandmother laughed. "A problem? David, the boys in our family had a special gift. They could all fart as much as they wanted, when they wanted. Sometimes they even farted at the kitchen table, especially after we'd had beans. With five boys in the family, and our father too, farting became a bit on the nose."

My grandmother cackled. I could hear her falsies rattling in her mouth.

I stared down at my feet.
I shook my head. I was

73

beginning to understand. There was no stink! There was no gut-turning stench! There was just a pleasant aroma.

My knees buckled at the thought.

I could almost smell the country freshness wafting round the hall as Wilma opened a Fart in a Jar during her school assembly. I could see Wilma's look of surprise as she caught a nostril full of something that wasn't Fart in a Jar.

The shame of it all.

"My mother was a smart woman," I heard my grandmother continue. "My mother discovered that a certain amount of a certain something in the food stopped the smell. My father and brothers could fart as much as they wanted, but for weeks, even months, after eating our mother's soup their farts were almost like bouquets of flowers. We ate a lot of soup in those days."

My grandmother paused and waited until I looked up at her. "Why do you ask?" she said.

I shrugged. I was already thinking about "Fragrance in a Jar", but somehow the name just didn't have the same promise to it. And I couldn't see Nick getting overly excited about it either, even if he survived his cousin Wilma.

It was back to the drawing board.

Or rather, it was back to basics. More beans. More eggs. And no more soup, of any kind. From now on I wasn't changing my diet for anyone.

For now though, I was just glad that I'd set a few of the original Farts in a Jar aside for emergencies. And this was definitely an emergency.

My grandmother was still explaining my ancestors' flatulence problems to me as I left the kitchen. I could hear her talking even as I returned from my room with a Force 5 jar in my hand.

"What's that, David?" my grandmother asked when I set the jar down next to the sink.

I grinned, unscrewed the lid and started backing out of the kitchen real fast.

I was at the door before I answered. By then my grandmother was leaning over the jar, peering into it. Her eyes were already watering.

"A family heirloom, Gran," I called back through a laugh. "Something passed down to me from the boys in the family."

From Archie Fusillo

I was lucky to go to school with a group of
guys who loved playing pranks. As a result,
my class was always into something or other,
usually at the expense of the poor teacher.
One popular prank was to wait until the
classroom was completely silent and then let
rip with a fart that shattered the air, and the
silence, and reduced everyone—teacher
included—to coughing fits and breathless
gasps. The idea to bottle and sell farts was
just too good an idea to pass up on, so...

From Stephen Michael King

Farting... What a stinky subject!

It's hard enough drawing something that's invisible, but I can't believe that I have to write something about it! My grandfather told me not to say a single word about him, so that put a stop to all my best fart stories. Anyhow I have to go because something around here really smells... It wasn't me... Maybe it was the dog... Yeah, the dog!... Hold on... What's that?... An empty jar...

HUNGry for more?

Have a Bite!